Beatrix F. Cresswell

The Royal Progress of King Pepito

Beatrix F. Cresswell

The Royal Progress of King Pepito

ISBN/EAN: 9783744617895

Printed in Europe, USA, Canada, Australia, Japan

Cover: Foto ©Andreas Hilbeck / pixelio.de

More available books at **www.hansebooks.com**

The Royal Progress

OF

KING PEPITO

BY

BEATRICE F. CRESSWELL

ILLUSTRATED BY

KATE GREENAWAY

ENGRAVED AND PRINTED BY EDMUND EVANS

LONDON
SOCIETY FOR PROMOTING CHRISTIAN KNOWLEDGE,
NORTHUMBERLAND AVENUE, CHARING CROSS. W.C.:
43, QUEEN VICTORIA STREET, E.C.
BRIGHTON: 135, NORTH STREET.
NEW YORK: E. & J. B. YOUNG & CO.

The Royal Progress

OF

KING PEPITO.

•••••••••••••••••••••••••••

THE Court of King Pepito was usually held in the nursery. It was a domain quite large enough for so small a person to reign over, though already he had great ambitions of spreading his conquests farther. Once already the fat legs had got as far as the top of the stairs, and King

B

Pepito had turned round to begin descending
backwards ; but nurse seeing him, caught him
with a shake that was half love, half punishment.
And Pepito took all the love, and never per-
ceived the punishment, but laughed in nurse's
face, and awaited another opportunity for setting
out on his travels. He had plenty of subjects
up there. The stout tabby cat who endured
most things, and the canary that sang when
Pepito took any notice of him. The rocking-
horse was a faithful steed who carried his
master gallantly ; and the woolly dog submitted
to being dragged about in any position, though
some of them must have been degrading, even
to the feelings of a woolly dog. Moreover, the
Pomeranian puppy had torn its head off,
ruining its beauty for ever. But Pepito loved
it still.

The wooden soldiers represented all the army
of King Pepito's realm, while the chief part of
the inhabitants were the animals from the Ark.

They were often taken into Pepito's bath — a
proceeding which must have horrified them, under
the impression that a second deluge was coming,
while the Ark stood high and dry on the Ararat
of the nursery table.

Then there was Kitty, faithful Kitty, who
always followed Pepito into mischief, sat with him
under the bed, and in the cupboard, or any other
dangerous situation into which Pepito's investi-
gating spirit might lead him.

Pepito had other courtiers known only to
himself. There were moments when, ceasing
playing, he would lift up his head, and with his
blue eyes fixed on vacancy, would see something
unseen by others, and hear voices audible to no
one else. Perhaps it was the fairies who had so
much to tell the little master as he sat upon the
nursery floor.

It was they who suggested him once more
attempting that dangerous journey downstairs,
when nurse was away in the kitchen. She had

left Pepito and the Pomeranian puppy together. The puppy was chawing up one of the animals from Noah's Ark, Pepito hugging the woolly dog.

Suddenly he heard those voices inaudible to every one else. For a moment he listened, then rose to follow them. Why he stopped an instant to take a wooden soldier no one will know. Perhaps he thought the officer might defend him, perhaps that he was going to spend a lifetime in Fairyland, and that kings ought not to travel without royal guards.

And the puppy came too.

As far as the top of the stairs the journey was easy enough, then difficulties arose. Pepito had to sit down and carefully turn round. He could only spare one hand to help himself with, the other clasped the soldier and the string of the woolly dog. So with difficulty he let himself down from step to step, the puppy running up and down all the while, hindering rather than helping his master, and the woolly dog bumped

all the way to the bottom. It must have been a painful journey for him.

How delightfully easy it was afterwards on the level ground! Kitty was sleeping in the hall, but the unusual sound of her little master's voice awoke her, and she followed him into the sunshine. Possibly the sight of the woolly dog dragging behind him attracted her—she was fond of careering after that much-enduring animal, as Pepito pulled him round the nursery table.

The roses on either side of the steps nodded "good-afternoon" to Pepito as he passed into the sunny garden. On the lawn the flowers were gleaming many colours in the beds. A butterfly flitting over them looked as though one of the blossoms had been detached from its stalk and given power of motion.

Pepito ran after it, but his activity did not equal the butterfly's. He fell down, and whilst occupied in the business of picking himself up again, Kitty raced forward after the cause of the

C

disaster.   A bound, a pat with those sharp paws, and there upon the grass lay a poor victim to royal caprice, and he, the monarch, heeds not at all that this innocent Becket should have perished to give him pleasure.

Over the grass they go, King Pepito, the puppy, and Kitty following the woolly dog.

King Pepito gathered flowers with fine disregard for rank.   Now a geranium, then a bright marigold, a rose that happens to be in reach, some daisies, buttercups which peep through the paling out of the hay-grass.   At present His Majesty's taste is gaudy, a poppy or glowing *Eschscholtzia* is of more value in his eyes than all the orchids ever grown, with their tender harmonious colouring.

Downhill ran the paths, and downhill trotted King Pepito.   At the foot of the hill the hay was cut in the meadow, and with the puppy in front to herald his coming, Pepito arrived amongst the haymakers.

He had been out but a little while, yet already his Court was more than doubled. The women threw down their rakes to pick him up, kiss him, and " bless his little heart." The men came over the long furrows to look at the little master. The gardeners left the hay to gather strawberries for him from the kitchen garden ; and they all took it for granted that nurse was coming, so they only made a house of hay for him under the spreading boughs of the elm-tree.

His Majesty was not unwilling to rest. The puppy was hot and panting, and King Pepito condescendingly fanned him with the cabbage leaf in which the strawberries had been. Pepito ate the juicy fruit, and the puppy finished up all the green husks, so that the hay house was quite tidy when they left it.

For they left it without giving any notice of their departure ; for where those fairy voices led, King Pepito was forced to follow.

He was not quite sure whether the green

caterpillar was not a fairy. She came down from the elm-tree in such a dangerous fashion, hanging to an almost invisible silk line, swaying to and fro under the breeze, and apparently not the least bit frightened. When she alighted on the hay at Pepito's side, he was rather alarmed, snatched the wooden soldier from beside her, for she was thinking of walking across him, and hurried away.

This piece of the journey filled the woolly dog with burrs. He was quite a pitiable sight when he reached the stream that ran through the meadow.

That stream was a joyful discovery to King Pepito. For several minutes he stood gazing at it too delighted to move. This was quite the most beautiful thing he had ever seen in his little life. Sparkling under the sunshine the stream rippled on, unaware of all the pleasure bestowed by its beauty. Over the pebbles it babbled, and then lay still in a tiny pool, then rippled on

again, every wavelet tipped gold with the sunshine. Along the banks the bitter-sweet, and
blue vetch festooned the wild roses, whose broad
white blossoms were spread wide to catch every
ray of sun. Here and there the meadow-sweet
was in flower, and where the haymakers' cruel
scythe had not come all the ground was sprinkled
with red sorrel flowers and white moon-daisies.

Then a water-wagtail came down to the
stones, and ran along them, wagging her tail up
and down, giving cunning looks at Pepito until
she saw Kitty, who frightened her, and she flew
away.

Pepito would rather have liked to follow her,
or to have gone with the swifts, that wheeling
round and round chased each other and uttered
their wild cries. Then a great stately gull passed
overhead with wings broad enough to have
carried King Pepito, at least so the child thought,
and for a moment was seized with a great wild
longing to go with him up into the blue sky.

Fortunately Pepito was not long occupied with things beyond his ken. The booming of a bumble-bee over a hard-head flower was enough to bring his thoughts from soaring away with the sea-gulls. Then splash, splash, a frog hopped across the stream and sat on a stone, his back glistening, and his bright yellow eyes looking towards the child.

"Come and see where I live," he seemed to say, and Pepito, nothing loth, accepted the invitation. Unfortunately he did not manage his progress from stone to stone as well as froggie, and fell into the water.

Rather a startling experience this, but Pepito had been wetter when he upset the nursery jug over himself. He scrambled up the other side of the bank, gave one rueful look backwards for the frog, who had totally disappeared, and then trotted on amongst the moon-daisies.

The path grows hilly, Pepito is following the upward course of the stream. The puppy prefers

walking in the water. Faithful Kitty has deserted her little master, crossing the brook was too severe a test for her loyalty. Upwards, ever upwards. What does Pepito see and hear that he so sturdily trots on, never pausing, never looking behind him, till the bushes close in on either side, the bracken fern rises over his head, and King Pepito has vanished into the realm of Faery?

Surely if Fairyland ever were found it would be some such place as this. Cool and green, with grassy banks sloping down to the stream-side, which bubbles and chatters over stones, green with waterweeds.

The hawthorns are old and gnarled, the ash-trees young and slender, rising up to the sun-shine, and hazel bushes complete the under growth. There has been a crop of blue-bells and primroses, which must have covered the ground; now a pale purple orchid rises here and there, rather mysterious-looking under the trees.

Pepito has smelt something sweet, it comes from a pale greeny-white flower, and eagerly he gathers it in his chubby hand.

Ah, those butterfly orchids, how they lead one on! From flower to flower, from bush to bush, Pepito goes ; he throws away the garden blossoms, and fills his hands with these sweet flowers.

Then with that sudden impulse which governs the habits of King Pepito, he sat down and gazed into the greenness, as though seeing the fairies swinging on the leaves.

See, there is a little commotion in the earth close by, a miniature earthquake, that stirs the ferns and mosses. Then out peeps a black head and queer little feet, and a mole makes its way out of the ground. It has no intention of adding itself to the courtiers of King Pepito, but busily grubs in the soft earth close by until it has again quite vanished. The puppy has looked on eagerly. If that queer thing had chosen to

attack Pepito, it would have flown at him, but under the circumstances, puppy is glad it has gone quietly away.

King Pepito sits very still, the wooden soldier falls from his hand into the stream. The puppy employs his time in picking the burrs from his fur, the woolly dog lies in a heap, a hopeless object, very wet, very muddy, and all over green burrs, which, poor fellow, he can't pick out for himself.

A rabbit peeped through the fern, but King Pepito was too still to frighten him, and so the little fellow stayed there nibbling at the fern whilst the sun travelled farther and farther round the hill, and began sinking down behind the big tors.

It was not so peaceful at home as in the goyle where Pepito was sleeping. Nurse had gone upstairs and found His Majesty fled away, and spent a good deal of time in calling for him all over the house, searching in all sorts of likely

D

and unlikely places, whilst King Pepito trotted down the garden path and made friends with the haymakers.

And they, when all distracted, the servants ran down to inquire of them, were so certain that he was resting in the hay castle, that it was a double shock to find he had disappeared from thence also. And nurse began crying and talking of gipsies, while the housemaid wondered if he could possibly be Pixie-led. And though the girl got well laughed at for her pains, it must be said that she was the wisest of them all. For who had been Pepito's guides in his wanderings if not the Pixies? There were pink clouds in the sky when Pepito's mother came driving home to meet a weeping nurse and hear, in answer to her inquiries, that King Pepito was lost.

Half laughing, half crying, she ran back to the hall, where stood Pepito's father and his godfather, whom they all unexpectedly had brought home with them.

"King Pepito is lost!" she cried. "Come and help us to find him."

. Down to the hay fields; there was no difficulty in tracing him so far. But beyond that it seemed a wilderness in which to look for a little boy. The hay was all cut and carried; the daisies and the sorrel were gone, only a dreary desert of stubble remained, with all the beauty vanished that it had worn during the afternoon.

But even as she looked his mother saw Kitty coming running and stumbling over the rough ground. Kitty had completely lost her way, and was very glad to see friends again.

"He has been here," the mother said, coming to the stream bank, where the traces of his fall were marked on the wet earth. •

And Pepito's godfather followed her, laughing at her sagacity. His father had gone searching in another direction.

"He will never find the child," she said. And up the hill she went till she reached the

golden broombush that barred the palace gate of
King Pepito.

"Can the little fellow possibly have come so
far?" his godfather asked.

"Look there," she said, in reply, pointing to
a red stick in the stream.

He fished it out. It was the wooden soldier,
rather the worse for his bath and the rolling over
rock and stone that he had undergone in being
washed down the stream.

Within the goyle it was dark and still. The
air was full of the scent of butterfly orchids.
The godfather sniffed and remarked upon it.
He was a botanist, and almost fancied that
he had seen *Bartsia viscosa* in the marshy field
outside. Thinking of that he stumbled over
the uneven ground, and did not see what was
to be seen till Pepito's mother drew his attention
to it.

A chubby little figure in a soiled white frock,
with socks slipped over the shoes, and torn

embroidery. One hand was full of butterfly orchids, the other clasped that long-suffering woolly dog. And scattered at his mother's feet was strewn a bunch of garden flowers.

A glow-worm, creeping through the moss at King Pepito's head, seemed intended by the fairies as a candle for His Majesty. The puppy, awakened by steps and voices, came wriggling towards them, making no noise, so as not to awaken King Pepito.

"Are you going to leave him here all night?" asked the godfather, smiling at the mother as she stood watching the scene.

"The darling! Fancy his coming all this long way!" was all she said.

Then she picked him up, and Pepito, opening his blue eyes, recognized who it was covering him with kisses.

"We've come here, mammy, me and puppy and Kitty and all," he murmured.

It was a mistake about Kitty, but King

Pepito fondly imagined that all his subjects were around him.

He had a sort of royal procession back to the house, borne in his godfather's arms, with the rest of his Court humbly following him.

And when he entered he was carried into the dining-room, there to eat strawberries and cream in triumph, because every one was too pleased to be angry with him.

For some time the centre of admiration, by-and-by people left off noticing King Pepito ; then the little head drooped and the long lashes sunk over the rosy cheeks, and King Pepito nodded like a poppy, till his mother seeing him, carried him off to bed.

When she returned the godfather began talking about him.

" There is a proverb," he said, " I don't know where it comes from, but it sounds Eastern : 'Where the King is there is the Court ; where the Master sits there is the head

of the table.' Do you notice its application to
King Pepito?"

She smiled.

"You must forgive us for making King
Pepito our lord and master just at present," she
said.

But the next day she went up to the goyle,
early in the morning when the dew was yet on
the leaves, and sitting there, she watched the
sunshine flickering through the branches and
resting on King Pepito's scattered bunch of
flowers.

And she thought of godfather's proverb, won-
dering where little King Pepito would lead his
Court in after life, and whether he would still be
so gentle and loving as to retain his empire and
mastery over all hearts. Then the proverb began
to take in her mind a sacred meaning, and she
thought of the King who rules over the whole
earth, Whose Court is in the heart of every one
that loves Him, of the Master who presides over